Curses With Benefits

AMY LAURENS

OTHER WORKS

Find other works by the author at www.amylaurens.com

Curses With Benefits

INKLET #99

AMY LAURENS

Inkprint
PRESS
www.inkprintpress.com

Print ISBN: 978-1-922434-45-6
eBook ISBN: 9798201559434

www.inkprintpress.com

National Library of Australia Cataloguing-in-Publication Data
Laurens, Amy 1985 –
Curses With Benefits
34 p.
ISBN: 978-1-922434-45-6
Inkprint Press, Canberra, Australia
1. Fiction—Fantasy—Urban 2. Fiction—Fantasy—Dark
Fantasy 3. Fiction—Short Stories

First Print Edition: February 2023
Cover photo © Zurijeta via Deposit Photos
Cover design © Inkprint Press
Interior art © Amy Laurens

CURSES WITH BENEFITS

Streetlights filtered in past the edges of the master bedroom's blinds, casting silvered bands up the wardrobe door in the dark. The air carried humidity from the shower, and the faint scent of sage soap lingered in the air. Harry lay drowsy and warm beneath the heavy covers on the bed, completely comfortable, and completely awake, even though the digital clock on the other side of the room said 2:00AM.

Unaccustomed to needing help falling asleep, Harry let his left hand dangle over the edge of the bed. "Seagal," he murmured. He inhaled, ready to name the big, black, Great Dane-shaped demon twice more to summon it—demon it may be, but its fur felt convincingly soft and sleek, and since he'd demonstrated to it quite convincingly that he had the ability to freeze its ears off if it set a toe out of line—

A skin-splintering shriek pierced the dark stillness of Harry's bedroom.

Seagal had appeared alright: on the floor to Harry's left, in the middle of a pitched, fervoured, violent battle with... something.

Claws flashed in the darkness.

Seagal's eyes glimmered like firelight. He shrieked again, an awful, bone-rattling cry, terror shaped into sound.

The thing attacking Seagal snarled, sending fear pulsing out into the night.

Heart pounding, hardly daring to move for fear of drawing attention to himself, Harry whispered, "Begone."

Seagal vanished, and the other creature—and the fearful, agonised shrieks.

Goosebumps pressed against Harry's fingertips where his right hand lay on his chest; the hair all up and down his arms had raised, and his heart pounded like he'd just finished running a hundred-metre sprint for his life.

Deep breaths. They're gone now. Deep breaths.

He inhaled through his nose, exhaled slowly through pursed lips, willing his muscles to relax just as when he woke from his occasional nightmares. (When you made a living hunting down the nastier of the supernatural entities in the world, occasional nightmares were the least you could expect.)

Nothing's hurting you.

The hairs on his arms and legs slowly settled, and the goosebumps diminished back to normal skin.

What *was* that thing?

And how powerful was it, that it could harm Seagal?

Adrenalin flashed through Harry's body for the second time as it occurred to him that actually, all he'd done in banishing Seagal was condemn him to fight alone.

Yes, alright, the demon dog with its cropped, pricked ears that trailed off into scribbles of coal black smoke and long, whip-like tail with the tuft of hair at the tip and elbow joints just a little too spiky, too angular was a *demon* dog...

But that didn't mean Harry had to abandon it. After all, the demon dog had never abandoned him.

He snorted briefly at that twist in fate; two years ago, he'd have frozen someone alive if they'd told him he'd come to feel empathy for the demon that dogged—ha ha—his footsteps like a personal black hole.

And yet—he sighed—here he was.

Harry dug his fingers into the slightly starchy sheet that covered his mattress. Inhaled deeply and let the warm, slightly savoury air ground his awareness. Licked his teeth, searching for the peppermint burn of his toothpaste. Strained his ears and caught the sound of a car whooshing past, a blackbird trilling its territorial night-time song, the faint hum of electronics.

And, thus grounded, Harry opened not his eyes, but his awareness, and let the primal energies of the earth flow through him.

Water was his strength, and that was easy to find with the air still thick with humidity; air was similarly plentiful. Fire came from the electrical currents pulsing through the house, earth from the rather aesthetic arrangement of dried wheat stalks he kept in a drinking glass half full of dirt on the dresser.

"Seagal," he murmured again. His muscles tensed instinctively—but his room stayed silent.

"Seagal!"

Nothing. And now his heart was pounding fearfully again—only this time the fear wasn't for him, but for his demon dog.

(His? When had Seagal become his?)

(Answer: when he'd been threatened by someone not Harry.)

"Seagal, Prince of Air and Night, Fleet of Foot and Master of Speed, Haunter of Shadows and Bringer of Sorrow, Seagal, Keeper of Lost Memories and Guardian of the Void, come forth!"

Harry had a split instant to realise he'd just shouted Seagal's full Name at the top of his voice at two in the morning, and that his neighbours a) might hear, b) would appreciate his weirdness even less than usual, and c) may possibly—infinitesimally small chance but still possible—have memorised that title, which would cause all sorts of problems if they tried to repeat it in the morning...

Seagal and his attacker burst back into the room.

Harry yelped and leapt off the bed to make room for them.

He stumbled, tangled in the blankets for a moment.

Seagal shrieked again, ear-splittingly loud.

The other creature snarled back.

Harry thumped to the ground—ow, carpet burn, left knee, ow—spun around as fast as possible in the middle of his floordrobe, and raised a hand.

"Aqua potentia!" he shouted in deliberately mangled Latin.

Phantom water jetted from his out-stretched hand and hit the two beasts currently tearing up his queen-sized bed with the force of a fire hose.

Seagal whimpered but, having suffered the brunt of Harry's water attacks before, otherwise simply rolled to one side and off the bed.

The other creature, however—something like what Harry imagined a wolverine (the creature, not the superhero) looked, if a wolverine weighed as much as he did—screamed in agony.

Perfect.

He'd taken a punt, but demons usually associated most closely with fire (being non-material creatures by nature, they used the elements to craft physical bodies for themselves when manifesting in the material world), making water his usual weapon of choice.

And behold: the wolverine demon's scream, equal parts pained and pissed off as Harry's phantom water attack continued gushing at it, was evidence that water had been a good choice.

"Begone!" Harry shouted over the screaming. "Begone, foul thing from the outer worlds! You have no place among this dwelling of mortals. Begone!"

Pain clamped down on his mind. And either the screaming stopped—or else Harry was now screaming so loudly that he couldn't hear anything else, because the demon had reached out with ephemeral claws, and had sunk them directly into his mind.

You dare, a furious voice intoned. *You* dare *interrupt* me.

Pain. Stabbing, seething, burning, furious pain.

Harry choked down his screams, gasped.

Never let them sense weakness.

"Yes," Harry hissed out through clenched teeth, every muscle in his body wound tight, hands fisting so his nails bit into his palms, thoughts clouded by the red mist of agony. "I dare."

A snarl.

The pressure in his head let up just a fraction as Seagal jumped the other demon where it towered on the bed.

Snarls. Yelps.

A flash of firelight from someone's eyes.

Harry raised his arm, trembling from the effort of moving through the burning grip of the wolverine demon, still holding fast to his mind.

"Aqua…" He gasped.

Seagal snapped at the wolverine— and his teeth found purchase, sinking deep into the wolverine's shoulder.

"Aqua potentia."

A shaky jet of ghostly water, silvery in the dark, shot against the wolverine

again, and the scent of dousing fire fil-
led the room.

River rocks.

Flowing water.

Something akin to a candle going
out.

The demon shrieked.

"Begone." Harry's arm fell to the
ground and he shook, exhausted,
spent.

The wolverine demon vanished.

Relief flowed through Harry's chest
like another wave of adrenalin as he
stared up at Seagal, now peering down
at him from atop the bed.

You saved me. Seagal's voice in Harry's head was firm, and decisive—and
carried only a hint of wonder around
its edges.

Harry tried a smile, made it halfway
and decided it was too much energy;
snorted softly instead. *Yo,* he said, too
tired to actually verbalise.

Seagal started down at him, fire-bright eyes unblinking as the air cool-ed around them.

Another car went past out front.

The blackbird dared another trill.

Seagal blinked. *You had trouble find-ing sleep.*

Harry nodded a fraction. The piles of clothes he was lying on were pretty comfortable, actually. And if he wasn't sleeping in bed, surely he could just... not move, and then not sleep equally as well down here.

The bed seemed like an awfully high thing to climb right now.

...Sleeping on a floordrobe wasn't *that* bad, was it? He was an adult. It was a legitimate choice he could make. ...Right?

Seagal nodded, one short, decisive movement. *You will find sleep,* he said, a little rumble in his voice. *For the next twelve months, nothing shall disturb your slumber, and neither shall slumber hide from you. Seek it,* he said, *and you shall find it.*

It was Harry's turn to blink. *I didn't know demons gave out blessings.*

Seagal's stare was long, and piercing, and Harry got the impression that if the demon had been able to make a dog mouth present a wicked, gleaming smile, he would have.

As it was, Harry was treated to a smile full of pointed teeth that glimmered in the filtered light of the streetlights.

Oh Harry, Seagal said. *We cannot.* He tilted his head in the manner of adorable dogs everywhere. *But sometimes we can offer curses with benefits.*

Seagal vanished.

The silence rang against Harry's ears.

He closed his eyes. *I'll get up in just a second,* he told himself—and snored.

As it turned out, sleeping on a floordrobe was a totally legitimate life choice, when you were an adult who'd had trouble falling asleep—and had just fought a moderately strong demon for the safety of a friend.

THE MAKING OF
CURSES WITH BENEFITS

Oh, Harry.

Let me explain: This story is a dream.

I mean that quite literally. The section from "A skin-splintering shriek" (p. 8) to "diminished back to normal skin" (p. 10) is very literally a dream that I had one night. And yes, I do frequently dream that I am someone else rather than myself, and yes, I dreamt I was a man named Harry.

In some ways, this was quite convenient: it was not long after the publication of *It All Changes Now,* a collection of flash fiction wherein I began making my way through a class full of delightful students' names in my stories. And there was a Harry I still needed a story for, and it did just seem to fit.

On the other hand... Another wizardly figure named Harry?

But every other name I tried just wouldn't stick, so in the end I gave up and ran with it.

Read more by Amy Laurens!

THE MULTIVERSE
MAY BURN

"That's enough." The judge, in her stylised white wig and long navy robes, didn't shout, but she didn't need to. Her gaze—not baby, not cornflower, not sky, but rather poison-dart frog, or cavernous ice, or man 'o war—over the top of her black-rimmed glasses was severe, the gaze of a woman who'd seen far too many trouble-makers in her life for even a molecule of sympathy to remain in her blood.

Alissa shivered. Before, she'd thought that maybe, if she'd come in with a good enough story and a water-tight argument, she might have had a chance. But that look from the judge brokered no compromise, and Alissa looked quickly away, studying the flecks of black in the white-marble floor tiles.

Tiny specks of silver shone, and for a moment Alissa thought that maybe they represented hope amid the black-and-white of the justice system. But that, surely, was too much to assume; the room stank of bleach so strongly they might as well have advertised, 'One courtroom, clean of germs and mercy both.'

Stomach twisting, Alissa raised her gaze to stare at the walls instead, more uncompromising white, except where the recording screens—panels as tall as she was, as wide as her arm-span—interrupted them.

Three of the viewing screens were currently in use. From one, a severe-faced man with salt-and-pepper hair and deep, deep lines in his dark skin frowned down at her. In another, the cyborg Natia Alchamp narrowed their hazel eyes, lightly-tanned fist clenching in front of them on the dark-wood desk they sat behind, occasional flares of colour coalescent around their head as they used their implant to access the multiverse.

And in the third…

Alissa swallowed heavily.

In the third, the most beautiful man she'd ever seen sat scowling at her, dark eyes full of something she could only assume was hatred. Two long, red scratches puckered his brown cheek and at the sight of them again, Alissa's stomach clenched, adrenalin punching through her system.

She could taste that blood in her mouth, metallic, sweet, and if anyone here thought she would ever be sorry for what she'd done, they had another thing coming.

She'd die first.

Literally, and they would be the ones to kill her.

Which, damn it all, it wasn't her *fault*. *They* were the ones who'd fed her mother Rapunzel in the first place, hoping for yet another super-powered child to join their ranks.

So how was it Alissa's fault if things had gone slightly wrong—assuming a spontaneous genetic mutation could be considered 'wrong'?

"It is obvious that you are as stubborn as you are articulate," the judge continued, as a school teacher disciplining an unruly child might. "But your arguments are irrelevant. The fact of the matter is that you not only possess the forbidden blood magic, you actively chose to use it on this man."

Alissa's nostrils flared. Curse Hannah. Curse the witches. Curse everyone involved with her birth—and most of all, herself. Alissa drew in a steely breath, the unforgiving bleach filling her awareness.

Well, so would she be. Unforgiving, resolved, and devoid of mercy. If they were going to sentence her to death for possessing a talent she hadn't asked for, didn't want, then by the Clans she'd go down swinging and take them all with her.

She snorted. Folded her arms. Raised her chin and stared back at the fair-skinned woman who thought herself worthy to lay judgement on this matter.

The judge narrowed her own eyes in return. "Well then, Alissa Fortuna McAlister. You have brought this fate upon yourself. You have admitted to wielding blood magic in an act of aggression against another human being, as if possessing the red magic wasn't bad enough—and we have seen recorded evidence that your magic glows red instead of blue, as it ought. You know the penalty for this is death."

Adrenalin pulsed again, this time with a sour squirt of acid in the back of her throat. Alissa coughed, trying to swallow away the burn.

This was it, then. This was the end,

and she'd take them all with her—

She felt both magics, the sanctioned blue and the unsanctioned red, rising in her body, one cold and sharp like a migraine, one hot and tingling like pins and needles, a metallic taste rising in the back of her throat like blood, if blood were copper-blue instead of iron-red.

She couldn't do anything about Raiden, who'd dobbed her in and thus effectively signed her death warrant himself, and that... well, that pissed her off, to be honest.

But the judge was going to be sorry.

"*Unless.*" The judge pursed her blue-painted lips, so bright they made her skin seem pale as death, so bright they outshone her gleaming eyes. "Someone will speak for you, and agree to complete a Multiverse Trial."

Keep reading! Head to
www.inkprintpress.com/
amylaurens/
itallchangesnow/
to buy your copy now!

ABOUT THE AUTHOR

AMY LAURENS is an Australian author of fantasy fiction for all ages. Her story *Bones Of The Sea*, about creepy carnivorous mist and bone curses, won the 2021 Aurealis Award for Best Fantasy Novella.

Amy has also written the award-winning portal-fantasy *Sanctuary* series about Edge, a 13-year-old girl forced to move to a small country town because of witness protection (the first book is *Where Shadows Rise*), the humorous fantasy *Kaditeos* series, following newly graduated Evil Overlord Mercury as she attempts to acquire a castle, the young adult series *Storm Foxes*, about love and magic and family in small town Australia, and a whole host of non-fiction.

INKLETS

Collect them all! Released on the 1st and 15th of each month.

Dancer, Dreamer Seer
LIANA BROOKS

As Time Whirls Slowly Past
AMY LAURENS

Far More Satisfying Than Hell
AMY LAURENS

Just Another Day In Hell
LIANA BROOKS

Moon and Morning
AMY LAURENS

Some Impropriety Expected
AMY LAURENS

NEON SNOW
LIANA BROOKS

Reincarnation
LIANA BROOKS

More Than Mushrooms
AMY LAURENS

DOUBLE ISSUE

How To Make A Star & The World Ended

LIANA BROOKS

CAUGHT IN THE ACT

AMY LAURENS

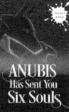

ANUBIS Has Sent You Six Souls

LIANA BROOKS

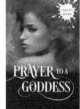

PRAYER TO A GODDESS

LIANA BROOKS

Love In The Time Of Corona

AMY LAURENS

RECRUITMENT

AMY LAURENS

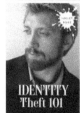

IDENTITY Theft 101

LIANA BROOKS

Curses With Benefits

AMY LAURENS

NECROMANCER TROUBLES

LIANA BROOKS

Lightning Source UK Ltd.
Milton Keynes UK
UKHW010839070223
416609UK00003B/1137